THE ANGRY MONK AND THE FLY

A TALE OF MINDFULNESS FOR CHILDREN

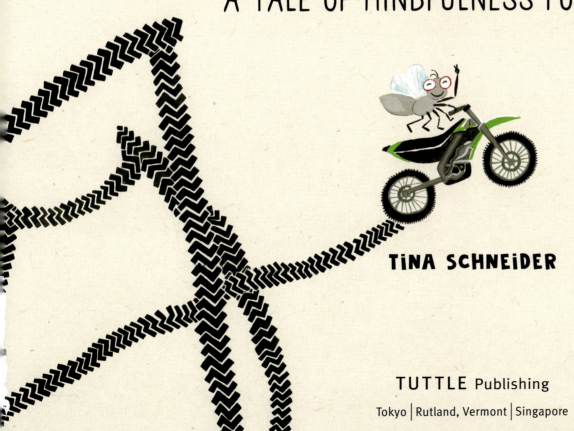

TINA SCHNEIDER

TUTTLE Publishing
Tokyo | Rutland, Vermont | Singapore

The monk sat in a field of morning glories.
He sat with crossed legs in robes the color of
orange dahlias.
The flowers turned to face him, as if
he were the sun itself.

He sat as still as a tree stump from
morning until night.
The wild animals were not afraid.
They knew this monk like nature, like weather and
earth know each other.

The animals curled up and slept at his feet.
They stretched out and basked in his peace.
All of their hearts were one with this monk.
All except one...

The Fly!

The fly had no respect for this monk.
He buzzed around his head like a tangle of yarn.
The monk tried to be still. He tried to be peaceful.
But inside his mind his anger rose like a flood,
until he couldn't take it anymore....
He swatted at the pesky fly and shouted,
GO AWAY!

The animals were startled from their peace.
They ran back to burrow and den.

Even the morning glories turned away.
The monk slumped in defeat,
That darn fly!

The monk was determined to do better.
The next day, he woke up before the sun.
He stepped gently between the sleeping flowers,
careful not to harm a single blade of grass.

He found a little clearing and took his seat.
He opened his hands like blossoms on his knees,
closed his eyes, and began to meditate.

Behind his closed eyes he saw his anger, still there, smoldering like a red hot ember. He tried not to pay attention to it.

Instead he focused on his breath.

Slowly his anger began to cool and drift out of sight,

like a pebble sinking below the surface of a lake.

Peace began to rise in him.

It rose up with the sun and darkness faded into a new day.

The wild animals flocked around the monk.

Peace spread throughout the land.

Chaos calmed into quiet.

Birds of every color encircled the monk like
a garland of flowers.
Their sweet song floated up and away on the breeze.
Noises everywhere were hushed.
Well...all noises...except one!

The fly zigged and zagged onto the scene like a tossed firecracker.

He zipped around the monk's head, buzzing loudly from ear to ear, as noisy as a flying motorcycle.

The monk's anger awakened like fire on dry wood.
It roared through his whole body,
until it was all he could see and all he could hear.
He clapped his hands together,
trying to squash that blasted fly, and yelled,
GO AWAY!

The quiet shattered like lightening.
All the birds burst back up into the trees.
All the animals fled.

Even the flowers closed up in fear.
The monk wilted in despair.
That dang fly!

Every day was the same.
The monk sat.
The animals gathered.
Peace rolled in like a white fog.
And then...
The fly showed up like a splat of black ink...

...staining the quiet with his one-insect band, sending our poor monk into a tizzy of frustration. Until one day...

The monk returned to the meadow.
He sat down to meditate.
The animals gathered.
Peace began to grow inside him and all around him.
And just like clockwork, the fly showed up.

But this time the fly didn't fly around the monk's head and criss-cross in front of his face. This time, the fly landed right on the tip of the monk's nose!

The monk opened his eyes just a slit.

His eyes crossed with anger when he saw
the fly sitting on his nose.
His anger boiled up and up like a kettle,
until his rage exploded and he shouted
at the top of his lungs, GO AWAY!
And they went away.
All the animals went far, far away.

And the monk was left alone.

All alone. Except for ... the fly!

The fly just sat on the tip of the monk's nose!

The monk was tired, too tired to be angry.

For the first time, he just looked.

He looked at the fly.

He looked really closely.

And what he saw surprised him.

He saw a thousand eyes looking back at him
And within each eye he saw himself.
And within each reflection of himself he saw the fly.
He saw Buddha-Fly!
And for a moment the world dissolved around him!

He was the fly and the fly was him.
They were one. They were the same.
There was no me and no you. No us and no them.
No anger. Only love.

And in that moment the monk could see
the vastness of the cosmos.
He could see every tiny detail of the earth
unfold like a map in his hands.

He was knowing beyond knowing
He was both the light and the darkness.
He was all beings and he was no one.
He was free.

He saw the fly.
He really saw him.
And the fly was beautiful.

The fly was Buddha-Fly.

to meditate:
sit comfortably
with your back straight
and your eyes closed

breathe easy

can you follow one breath?

when does it begin?

where does it end?

watch yourself breathing
inhaling
and
exhaling

belly and chest
rise
belly and chest fall

if your mind wanders
say hello to your thoughts
like waving to a
friend in a crowd

then let them go

return your attention
to your breath
again
and
again

be gentle with yourself

smile

This book is for my teachers.

"Books to Span the East and West"

Tuttle Publishing was founded in 1832 in the small New England town of Rutland, Vermont [USA]. Our core values remain as strong today as they were then—to publish best-in-class books which bring people together one page at a time. In 1948, we established a publishing office in Japan—and Tuttle is now a leader in publishing English-language books about the arts, languages and cultures of Asia. The world has become a much smaller place today and Asia's economic and cultural influence has grown. Yet the need for meaningful dialogue and information about this diverse region has never been greater. Over the past seven decades, Tuttle has published thousands of books on subjects ranging from martial arts and paper crafts to language learning and literature—and our talented authors, illustrators, designers and photographers have won many prestigious awards. We welcome you to explore the wealth of information available on Asia at **www.tuttlepublishing.com**.

Published by Tuttle Publishing, an imprint of Periplus Editions (HK) Ltd.

www.tuttlepublishing.com

Text ©2022 Tina Schneider
Illustrations ©2022 Tina Schneider

All rights reserved. No part of this publication may be reproduced or utilized in any form or by any means, electronic or mechanical, including photocopying, recording, or by any information storage and retrieval system, without prior written permission from the publisher.

Library of Congress Control Number: 2022934243

Isbn: 978-0-8048-5375-0

DISTRIBUTED BY

North America, Latin America & Europe
Tuttle Publishing
364 Innovation Drive
North Clarendon VT 05759-9436 U.S.A.
Tel: 1 (802) 773-8930
Fax: 1 (802) 773-6993
info@tuttlepublishing.com
www.tuttlepublishing.com

Japan
Tuttle Publishing
Yaekari Building 3rd Floor
5-4-12 Osaki
Shinagawa-ku
Tokyo 141-0032
Tel: (81) 3 5437-0171
Fax: (81) 3 5437-0755
sales@tuttle.co.jp
www.tuttle.co.jp

Asia Pacific
Berkeley Books Pte. Ltd.
3 Kallang Sector #04-01
Singapore 349278
Tel: (65) 6741 2178
Fax: (65) 6741 2179
inquiries@periplus.com.sg
www.tuttlepublishing.com

25 24 23 22   10 9 8 7 6 5 4 3 2 1

Printed in Malaysia   2204TO

TUTTLE PUBLISHING® is a registered trademark of Tuttle Publishing, a division of Periplus Editions (HK) Ltd.